This Winnie-the-Pooh
book belongs to

. . . .

EGMONT

We bring stories to life

First Published in Great Britain 2019 by Egmont UK Limited
The Yellow Building, 1 Nicholas Road, London W11 4AN

Written by Jane Riordan
Designed by Pritty Ramjee
Illustrated by Eleanor Taylor and Mikki Butterley

Copyright © 2019 Disney Enterprises, Inc.
Based on the "Winnie the Pooh" works
by A.A.Milne and E.H.Shepard

ISBN 978 1 4052 9462 1
70395/002
Printed in Italy

Stay safe online. Egmont is not responsible for content hosted by third parties.

Egmont takes its responsibility to the planet and its inhabitants very seriously.
We aim to use paper from well-managed forests run by responsible suppliers.

Winnie-the-Pooh
A Pudding for Christmas

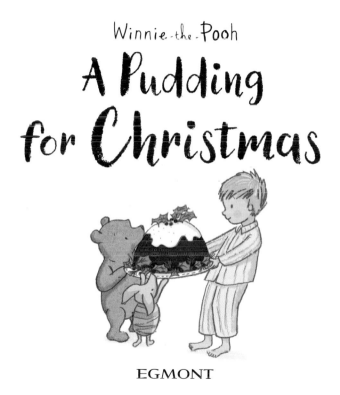

EGMONT

The days were short, and the evenings were long and cold. Christopher Robin had laid his dominoes all around the room and read all his books from front to back and then back to front. He pressed his nose up against the cold, squeaky glass.

"Pooh will know what to do," he thought to himself and he stepped out into the Forest.

"Who's there?" came a *sleepy* voice from the other side of the door.

"Me," called Christopher Robin.

"Can't be," came the reply.

"Open up, Silly Old Bear," sighed Christopher Robin.

"Oh, it's **you**," said Pooh, letting him in. "I thought it couldn't be **me**."

Christopher Robin was just asking Pooh what to do, when Pooh said: "Food!"

"Food?" asked Christopher Robin.

"Food means friends and friends mean food and that's all there is to it," Pooh said, wisely.

And so, word was sent out that
everyone was to gather
for a feast.

"We'll make a **pudding!**" announced Christopher Robin. "A gigantic, delicious pudding, as **big** as Pooh."

At this, Pooh blushed with quiet pride and stuck out his round tummy in an important sort of way.

Everybody helped with the pudding.

Pooh **poured** in honey.

Piglet and Roo **tipped** in currants.

Tigger **bounced** in eggs.

Owl **sifted** flour and spice.

And Eeyore **offered** words of advice and caution.

"Now we all stir the pudding and make a wish," explained Christopher Robin. "But, if you tell anyone your wish, it won't come true."

One by one the friends gave the pudding a stir.

Christopher Robin **wished** he was twice as tall. Owl **wished** he could spell 'del ... deli ... deliciouss.' Pooh **wished** he was eating the pudding already. Rabbit **wished** the queue was a little more orderly.

Piglet **wished** that Woozles ... weren't. Tigger **wished** he knew what making a **wish** was. Eeyore **wished** Tigger wouldn't bounce on his ear.

And Kanga was about to make her wish when ...

"Where's Roo?" she gasped.

Christopher Robin
looked **high**.

And Pooh looked **low**.

 Piglet looked in small places.

And Eeyore looked between his legs.

But little Roo was **nowhere** to be seen ...

"I fear the pudding may have got him," ventured Eeyore. "I always knew that no good would come from such a **large, sticky pudding** ..." he trailed off as, **horrified**, everyone looked towards the enormous mixing bowl.

"Roo?" squeaked Kanga,

"Are you in there, dear?"

At once, Rabbit took charge.

"At a time like this," he announced, importantly, "I would strongly suggest," he continued, "that the pudding should **not** be cooked."

Kanga began to wobble a little and had to be sat in a comfortable chair.

"**Hush!**" said Eeyore in a serious voice.
"I hear a sound."

Everyone hushed, and it was true; there was
a very small sound, but it was certainly a
sound ... a sort of **snoozing** sound.

The sound came from a corner and there they
found Roo, fast asleep among the currants.
It seemed that he had eaten a great many and
the effort had tired him out.

With Roo found and the pudding steaming, the friends noticed that a great deal of it seemed to be on their noses and paws ...

"Bathtime," said Christopher Robin. But if the truth be told, the washing was almost as messy as the cooking!

Meanwhile, a **wonderful** smell had started to drift out from the kitchen. It was a smell of fruit and spice and ... *Christmas.*

"The pudding is ready!" announced Christopher Robin.

It was the **finest** pudding they had ever seen. Only Eeyore couldn't be persuaded to try some.

"Call me fussy if you will," he complained. "But that pudding has had too many paws (and tails) in it, if you see what I mean."

Christopher Robin found Eeyore a thistle and the friends settled down to enjoy their feast.

"If a **wish** has already come true," asked Pooh thoughtfully, as he licked the last few crumbs from his plate, "can you tell it?"

But nobody replied ... for they were all fast asleep.

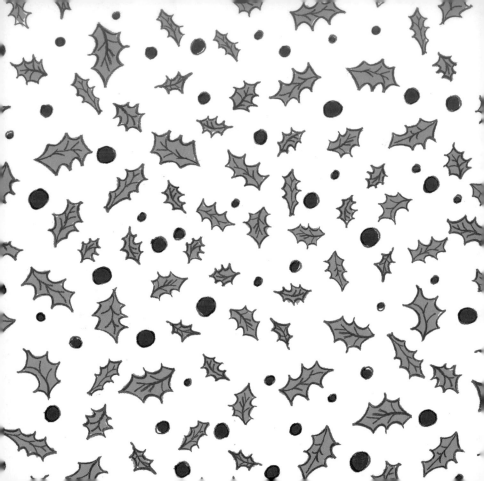

Enjoy other wintery tales with Winnie-the-Pooh and friends!

A Tree for Christmas
ISBN 9781405286633

The Long Winter's Sleep
ISBN 9781405291095